BLIND
MAN'S
BLUFF

BLIND
MAN'S
BLUFF

AIDAN HIGGINS

DALKEY ARCHIVE PRESS
CHAMPAIGN • DUBLIN • LONDON

ANECDOTES, CARTOONS, COLLAGES, and PICS

For the Semi-Blind

Compiled with the Aid of Neil Donnelly,
Matthew Geden, and Alannah Hopkin.

Part the diamonds and you'll find slug's meat.

Djuna Barnes

Library of Congress Cataloging-in-Publication Data

Higgins, Aidan, 1927-
Blind man's bluff / Aidan Higgins.
    p. cm.
ISBN 978-1-56478-725-5 (pbk. : alk. paper)
1. Higgins, Aidan, 1927---Notebooks, sketchbooks, etc. I. Title.
PR6058.I34Z4635 2012
823'.914--dc23

                    2012012749

Partially funded by a grant from the Illinois Arts Council, a state
agency

www.dalkeyarchive.com

Cover design and composition by Sarah French; artwork by Aidan
Higgins

CONTENTS

BLIND
MAN'S
BLUFF

Flood and Fire

Nothing was ever as familiar as the mile-long road from our front gate (two lodges, seventy-two acres, grazing for horses or cows) to the village a mile off. It seemed forever in existence and could never change. At the corner was Brady's farm. Next was the Collegiate Girls' School. The Protestant orphans seemed to spend most of their free time in the hockey field instead of the classroom. They were taken crocodile-fashion in double file for walks at regular intervals, their teachers striding behind. I was acutely embarrassed when I had to pass this file of chattering girls, and blushed to the roots of my hair.

One day came a strange disruption of the ordinary. As usual I was being pushed in my black-hooded pram, that most funereal looking thing, into the village and found water up to the approaches of Marlay Abbey, then occupied by nuns. The village was flooded, the Liffey had overflowed its banks, the bridge with five arches was under water. No one was about. We had to turn back. What must the deluge have been like? It was a day of prodigious happenings, never to be repeated. Nothing predictable was to be expected. It was to become a time of stupendous occasions. First the flood, then the death of the postman and old Jem Brady.

For days it was noticed that he behaved peculiarly, he wasn't himself. Then one morning his bed was empty.

My Mother and the Cat

Years went by and Papa Hemingway hobnobbing with Castro in Cuba had tamed an owl for which he could find no adequate pet name. Papa was a great inventor of cruel nicknames, called Marlene Dietrich "the Kraut." Not finding a suitable pet name for the owl, he called it OWL, wise old owl, and this suited the bird as no other name could. No other word would do.

You might like to know how it all began, what induced me to write in the first place. Why, where everyone began, with one's mother, herself a voracious reader, with access to banned books. The light romance, *Without My Cloak*, and Brinsely McNamara's *The Valley of the Squinting Windows* that my wife wittily renamed *The Valley of the Squinting Widows*.

My mother put a pencil in my hand and pointed at the cat that was watching us intensely, and said, "Write down

CAT for me in capital letters." She tried for days to get me to write CAT but I could feel no affinity between the observant dumb creature and the word CAT. My mother tried Hat, Fat, Mat, Bat, all to no avail, until one day the miracle occurred. Animate and inanimate merged. I could now make the connection between words and a living being.

Eventually my mother's patience was rewarded, and I could read Christopher Robin and the likes. In a few years I had advanced to *Robinson Crusoe* and would never look back.

My mother took me to a garden sale of books in Marlay Abbey and I came away with Hemingway's *Green Hills of Africa*, while she confined herself to Beverley Nichols's *Down the Garden Path*. Voracious readers will read anything, from trash to profundity.

Later, I contracted measles, which was duly passed on to my younger brother, dead before me like my two elder brothers. The curative for measles in those far-off times was to put the boy to bed for six weeks in a darkened bedroom and let him amuse himself as best he could.

My mother, the great reader, went to a Dublin bookshop and bought Hans Christian Andersen. I was away.

Education With the Nuns

One day, long dreaded, we were committed to the tender care of the nuns to begin our formal education. We walked the mile from our grand mansion, mother and two bewildered lads, and were formally received at the convent by the Reverend Mother in person. Education is so important, my mother opened proceedings, and offered the Reverend Mother a Zube which was formally accepted in a gesture of good will.

Time passed and we became acclimatized to our fellow-sufferers. One day passing the girls' cloakroom I saw a couple of white enamel bowls brimming with girlish blood, only recently extracted, and guessed that the visiting dentist had been at his rough and ready trade. About the playground they passed, pale and wan, handkerchiefs bloodied.

LAYING AN EGG

Road Kill

Tim Timmons it was who carried the post for Colonel Clements, and lost his life while on the job. He was a familiar sight cycling between the Clements' long avenue and the village below. One day he got on his bike to catch the Birr bus coming from Dublin. The avenue terminated at the end of the hill, as did the life of the popular postman under the wheels of the six o'clock bus carrying passengers home to their tea. The lads in our front lodge who liked to tell a tall tale gave us a gruesome account of the collision, the blood and guts of the unfortunate postman, the clearing up of the mess of the dead Timmy Timmons. Buckets of water flung down the hill, and yard brushes applied vigorously. Nurse kept the pram clear of the accident. It came to us as hearsay, the death of the soft-spoken postman. Not long after, while I was being conveyed down the Clements' long woody avenue, a blackbird fell dead alongside the pram, gazed at with wonder by my brother, aged two, who commented "Finished," the first word he ever uttered, acknowledging with wonder the world he found himself in. Nurse said it was the ghost of the dead postman. Such superstition was rife down our way. Death was always near in Celbridge.

CNESS ON BURRIANA

The Suicide of Old Jem Brady

My lackadaisical father, as lazy as they come, ran a stable for racehorses. *Cabin Fire* and *One Down* come to mind, the latter well named because he was never placed. My father was in the front yard when who should show up but our near neighbour old Jem Brady. Always garrulous, my father remarked, "Yesterday I saw a rat in one of the stables." The taciturn farmer didn't reply for a while. Then he said, "Of all the birds in the air, I do hate a rat." This became a stock phrase in our family.

Old Jem's behaviour became odder and odder; then one morning his bed was found empty. The early riser had not risen. A vigilant guard noticed footsteps in the morning dew, leading to the quarry with its reputation of being depthless. But nothing came up in the net. One last trawl of the net before lunch and up came the drowned farmer. My young brother and I cycling to school flew past the death quarry, a bluish gas hovered over the last resting place of the good farmer, much mourned and long remembered. Thus ended childhood.

1882 — 1941

Jesuit Casuistry

Sunday was visiting day at Clongowes Wood College and my father encountered Fr. Gerald O'Byrne, familiarly known as Gerry Razz, a scholar of classical Greek who had been in the Spanish Civil War and was spat on by a fascist, one of those who stabled their horses in Spanish churches and desecrated the holy statues. How the fascist beast reacted is not known, the pugilist must have beaten the anti-Christ to a pulp. Gerry Razz and my father had been companions in Longford at the start of their careers. In prep school we were read *Hiawatha* by the Captain of the school, placed in a chair where two classes could hear him. Da asked what do the J's make of James Joyce? He did not appear in the Collegium of past alumni. "We're not proud of him," told all. I left Clongowes Wood College ignorant of the difference between Lord Haw-Haw and James Joyce. Jesuit education was all about religion, Mass followed by Holy Communion followed by Confirmation.

Lord Nelson's Hat

On a winter afternoon in London, one of those grey life-less days you get there, I was making my way through Trafalgar Square and looking up at the grey sky noticed a small flag flying on top of Nelson's column. Other pedes-trians seemed to have noticed it too, for they were looking up and discussing it as they passed along, and I thought "How amazing—people are becoming observant and taking note of their surroundings at last." But hold on, this was back in the bad old days when the other Nelson, Mandela, was still breaking rocks on his penal island, and two intrepid South African climbers had scaled the tall column and stuck a South African flag on Horatio's high hat as an anti-Apartheid gesture. There was a photograph on the front page of the *Evening Standard* to prove it, and this is why the people were staring up, confirming what the paper had shown: there was an anti-Apartheid flag stuck on top of Nelson's foppish yet natty naval hat. Now what was one to make of that? Who would take it down? (Do not come down the ladder; I have taken it away.) It took the British Army to get it down, the engineers to remove it.

My three sons were raised in north London, in Muswell Hill Broadway, where they attended schools within sight of Alexandra Palace which had been set on fire thrice, the last time during a Parents' Meeting held in a house overlooking the park. The kids rushed to the window and shouted "Hey look, Mum, Alexandra Palace is on fire!" They wanted to run home to see it on the six o'clock news.

The planting of the flag on Nelson's hat, a symbolic gesture, a metaphor, wasn't real until confirmed by a photo on the front page of the *Evening Standard*—and a palace going up in flames and smoke wasn't real until the kids had seen it on television news, to authenticate it. One summer the pavements of Muswell Hill Broadway were crawling with ladybirds and nobody noticed them.

Handy Andy

We encountered him on the train to Barcelona—the *Talgo*—on our way out of France—Port Vendres in the Pyrenees in our case, and somewhere deeper in the mountains for him whose name I forget. He had an eye injury from an accident with a van going on the wrong side of the road, or so he said. He regaled us with many a strange tale. He had trouble recalling our names and called us Jacob (pronounced Yacob) and Marlene. Andy Hand, familiarly known as Handy Andy, as a lad had lost his right hand from the wrist down, and his left thumb, letting off fireworks, the missing hand replaced with a colossal crook. He ran a fish and chip shop in Kinsale, to where he was bound. He was barred from most of the hostelries in Kinsale where the villainous-looking crook was an object of common fear. One day he did a runner and was never seen again.

Compass Hill

We live in a two-storey house at No. 2 Higher Street, Kinsale, which has two other No. 2's, which makes three in all. No shop blemishes Compass Hill, above our street, and it's a mile or more into town. Walking around Compass Hill, you pass through all four points of the compass. You can see north, east, south, and west. Two suicides occurred there.

Three new identical mansions have been erected in our time here. From the middle one a suicide drove his car over the cliff at the Old Head to his death on the boulders below. He was deluded into believing that his business was ruined, but it wasn't, and he had gone away into whatever lies below.

Fiddler's Well, the next house on Compass Hill, is named for a fiddler who fiddled in the wet field, perhaps in the time of war or earlier. It is named after another suicide, a desperate man who threw himself to his death there. How deep was the well, though, or how shallow? Did he drown or break his neck in shallow water? It is not as easy as it seems. Doing away with oneself is a serious business. Twice I have attempted suicide, plunged in deep despair, once in Berlin, overlooking Schlachtensee lake, where an RAF bomber was shot down and not recovered to this day, despite the best efforts of French divers: half bottle of vodka to anaesthetize me, and intended to slash my ankles, but drank the vodka and went home; and once in our home garden, under the apple tree armed with a kitchen knife, watched by a black cat, omen that the end is nigh—*Naseby*, whose life I had saved as a kitten.

Suffer the little children to come unto me.

A Tiff with Mary Ann Quigley

Her moods were as unpredictable as the Irish climate itself, kind to strangers, not so amiable to locals. She was a small stout person, claimed that she never barred a customer, but gave them the cold shoulder instead. Her son James was a quiet lad who sometimes helped in the bar. Her husband, Kipper, was a fisherman, whom she treated like a dog. Because of earlier misdemeanours, Kipper was forbidden the lounge bar. Enduring the cold shoulder of relegation to a fish shed, his life cannot have been an easy one. The Quigleys never walked out together or showed each other any sign of affection.

For no particular reason she had it in for me, in the rude vernacular; I was stuck up and was getting the cold shoulder. I made no friends in her bar, nor brought in new friends. I was a liability more than anything else. We had disliked and distrusted each other from the start.

And now it was her turn to get even, when I entered the

Fishy Fishy Bar with bloodshot eye and vacillating tread, for that morning I had received no less than three injections in the left eyeball, and must have resembled Wild Bill Hickok after a good morning's buffalo-slaughtering.

"I need a drink," I said. She regarded me with deep suspicion. "I'm not going to serve you," she said (pause for affecting leery look). "If a Guard came in and saw you . . ." She left the rest unsaid. But she didn't serve me. She was assiduously pulling pints and making sure not to catch my bloodshot eye.

I felt someone behind me, her son James, warned that mischief was afoot. "The bitch won't serve me," I told him to his face.

"Now you've gone too far, calling my mother a bitch. You're barred here."

"You say those you dislike won't be served? A blackamoor, a dwarf?"

"This is the law," he said.

"You can't call a woman a bitch," called out a tall American visitor at the counter's end.

"Stay out of this; it's none of your business. Americans in foreign lands should keep their mouths shut. Bush should keep his trap shut too, otherwise he will lead us into another war."

In the Psychiatric Ward

The staff had a masterly command of psychological jargon. Passing the front office one morning I hear one of them reprimand a patient:

"Two showers in one morning. That's paranoid!"

The notice read CLINICAL WASTE.

"What's this your name is again?"

In a set of white plastic mugs lined up on the windowsill overlooking the drenched car park I am identified as A. HIGGS. At least I think it must refer to me, not B. MUGGS.

David Lordan asked me, twice, whether I was a fisherman. No, I told him. "You look like an artist," he said. I heard him tell one of the Filipino cleaning women that he was a stonemason; to Dr. Margaret Madden he was a sculptor.

I asked him did he know the work of Scanlon who had

erected a stone group of pyramids with stained glass windows let into them, in Sneem. No, he didn't.

"He's a sort of religious freak," I said. "A believer in an age of unbelief."

"I too am a religious freak," said Lordan.

"What form does your freakishness take?"

"I am the Holy Ghost."

"That's freakish alright."

Once the Holy Ghost gave me a curious handshake, a dry Masonic touch, the thumb used as the tongue in a French kiss.

Features of the place were:

(a) No mirrors

(b) Night and day staff were male to a man

(c) Head guru (Dr. Hannah Hannigan) was certainly the female in charge.

Volunteers, acting as a sort of street criers, walked into the wards at the appropriate times calling out: "Communion!"

"Confession!"

"Medication!"

"Mass!"
And most mellifluous of all,
"TEA-TIME!"

Small dumpy nuns in mufti distributed Holy Communion to the faithful. The sisters might have been offering Häagen-Dazs. Sometimes a priest came on his rounds, again in mufti, no sign of a Roman collar.

Somebody in the front office—perhaps Hannah herself—must have complained of David Lordan going about in dressing gown and pyjamas; because his apparel changed radically one day—black leather pants tightly fitted, studs, a decorative vest—the Rock Star incarnate.

One morning awaiting "meds" distribution after breakfast I took a stroll with Lordan along a glassed-in corridor and he mentioned once again that he was the Holy Ghost, showing me some religious emblem about his neck that I couldn't see due to my poor eyesight. I looked into his eyes and saw nothing, saw that there was nobody home, the house was empty.

"David Lordan thinks he is the Holy Ghost," I told Dr. Madden.

"David Lordan thinks he is many things," she said.

He had walked about in night attire all day long. Lord Fop in carpet slippers, dressing gown, and pyjamas. As likely as not silent with those who addressed him, disappearing down the back stairs to the smoking area below. Smoking was strictly forbidden in the ward, but I have heard the surreptitious scrape of a match at night, when all were asleep, and smelt the whiff of nicotine.

Shortly after being voluntarily admitted by a Doctor Yap I was summoned downstairs to be interviewed by Head Guru Dr. Hannah Hannigan where I failed to make a good impression. We were not long in the interview when Dr Hannigan was good enough to inform me that I was the suicide type, to which I responded:

"You are a very stupid woman. There is no such *type*. Two of my best friends, threatened with cancer, topped themselves and neither were the suicide *type*. One overdosed in St. Amour, the other shot himself with a point two-two rifle in a wood in British Columbia."

Dr. Madden was taking notes assiduously to Dr. Hannigan's right.

"You might just as well say that Dr. Madden here is the suicide type."

Dr. Madden imparted a secret smile in my direction.

"We may come from the same part of the country, but that does not necessarily make us the same sort of person. No, we are all different," I said. "I belong to that curious category—the non-suicide type—given to making gestures with a blunt knife under an apple tree. Vague gestures. We differ as much as different types of dogs, Greyhounds and Rottweilers, Alsatians and Pekinese."

"All dogs belong to the same species," said Dr. Hannigan, "All are canines."

"I meant different types," I said. "Savage or sweet-natured, big or small, amenable or saucy."

Dr. Madden wrote down *saucy* and underlined it. Dr. Hannigan began preparatory moves for ending the interview, putting away papers into her briefcase.

"We'll leave it there," she said. "Dr. Madden and I shall be seeing you again. If I can be of help in any way let me know."

Once, leaving my bed, half-asleep, I fell unconscious on the floor. I had a period of falling unconscious and two days of the shits from food poisoning. An attempt was made to deprive me of sugar with my porridge, given the mistaken notion that I was a diabetic. Breakfast over, the

Filipino women set about cleaning up. A girl with big wobbly breasts in her loose nightgown sat opposite slurping milky tea like a calf at the milking pail. The women scarcely spoke to each other, breakfasting in silence and departing without a word, wrapped up in their troubles, whatever they might be.

You must never ask—*When can I leave?*
  The Doctors do not like this question; it is for them to decide. What are the saddest words in the language?
  Punishment,
  Pleading,
  Homelessness,
  leaving aside all manner of illness, and finally,
  Death!

Returning from lunch (Spaghetti Bolognese) one day I spoke to a patient dressed to leave, sitting in the reception area. He told me that he had been in before.
  "I am a Psychotic," he said.
  "And now you are cured?"
  "I'm as right as rain."

And after three weeks internment I myself was free to go. It was pouring rain in the car park, as it had been when I arrived.

Postscript: The joy of returning home with Zinna in the Peugeot after the kindest possible treatment from Doctors Hannigan and Madden; others too, not forgetting the Filipino woman, Zip, not forgotten. The rudeness or downright insult taken on the chin from a retort by an impatient patient who is not suicidally inclined but was at least unbalanced, temporarily at least, was forgiven by Dr. Hannigan.

Goodbye to porridge.

Pachanga!

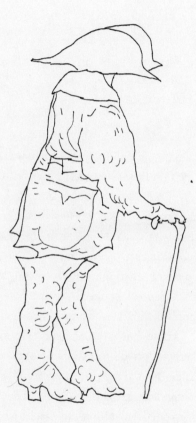

Reverse →

The Enigmatic Publisher John Calder

Calder is a difficult man to describe. He was short of stature. Had he thin lips? Grey eyes? He gave the impression of greyness. Calder was wealthy, inherited wealth from timber and Scotch whiskey I believe. His clothes were expensive, but with defects—a tear in the jacket shoulder. He married a Yugoslav opera singer—whom he called the Bosnian peasant, after the divorce—who, the dogmatic John Beckett claimed, could not read a note of music: an unlikely conjunction. He was a reckless spender. He was difficult to know, but good at heart. He found Samuel Beckett, and published several other Nobel Prize winners.

John Calder invited my wife, myself, and a Swiss beauty with revealing cleavage to his London apartment. I had only recently been fitted with bi-focal spectacles which instead of improving my eyesight had the opposite effect, as presently became apparent when, replacing my glass of Sancerre but missing the table edge by inches, I smashed the glass on the floor. Towards the end of the meal coffee was served, and I misplaced the table and smashed the coffee cup.

I remember my mother saying it was rude to point. I say it is rude to count.

Calder the opera enthusiast had attended over three thousand performances of some eight hundred different operas. He records the details of every single performance in five volumes of opera diaries. "And how many wenches have you had yourself?" For Calder, apparently, counting his conquests was a cure of insomnia. When he couldn't sleep he made a mental list. Calder the soft-spoken Scots cocksman counted three hundred past lovers, which I have no reason to doubt. He is after all a Scotsman and randy as James Boswell. Pray, recall Boswell's encounter with two young whores on London Bridge, or the actress whom he took to a hotel outside the city. Five times he had her in one night. "Sir, you are a prodigy of nature," was her coy response to this priggishness. "How many times then, would be right and proper?" asked the insatiable Scot. "Twice," she said.

He was a peerless publisher but not a sharp business-man. Witness how the Bosnian Peasant deprived him of his grouse moor and shooting lodge in the divorce proceedings. He was sometimes tight with royalties though the last time he visited me he brought two bottles of wine.

Contretemps in the Chinese Restaurant

The Chinese Restaurant was sparsely populated except for a couple of Cork men rather loudly discussing private affairs, as is the way with Corkonians. One was stout, the other was smoking. Tobacco fumes were annoying me, a non-smoker.

"Smoking to me is as offensive as farting."

I heard the sound of an unseen diner behind me. Having supped, he rose up and marched past our table, remarking "They shouldn't let drunks like that in here," which brought a smirk to the stout affronted Cork man, pleased that I was put in my place.

Not satisfied with this parting shot, the Cork man shouted out "Isn't he the crusty old cunt!" The portly Cork man smirked, satisfied that the upstart had been put in his place.

My response wiped the smirk off the fat-faced Cork man. "He has a queer notion of gender if he thinks men have one. Though I wouldn't put it past you."

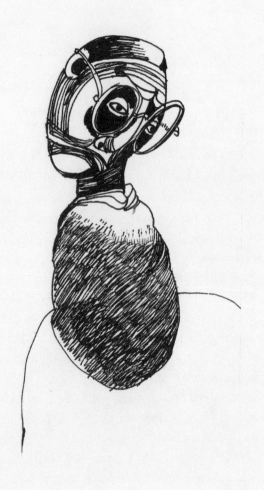

The Japanese Intruder

It was an unusually hot day in August with the sun going in and out as is its customary way in this erratic island climate. I had a gin and tonic to hand and was reading John Cheever's *Falconer* when the sun was obliterated. I strolled to the vegetable quarter abutting on the Protestant cemetery overlooked by the 11th-century church tower. As I came to the cemetery wall, drink in hand, I espied across the cemetery a small grey-clad figure in the arbour opposite. When he saw me watching he retreated into the dimness of the archway, only to reappear presently and stare across as blatantly as before. The sun came out, I retreated drink in hand to my Cheever. Presently a figure rushed through the tall ferns, a camera round his neck, and reappeared in the arbour. "I think you are in the wrong garden," I called out to the intruder, whereupon he reappeared, bold as brass. "I *know* you are in the wrong garden," I called out to him. I tried four languages but his response was bewilderment. "Japanese?" I suggested. "You are Japanese?"

Did you ever see a Japanese without his camera? Did you ever see one alone? They seem to travel in packs, snapping away at this or that, anything that takes their fancy. They are an odd race, to be sure.

I led the trespasser up into the house, surprising my wife stark naked after a shower. The bold intruder pretended not to notice, jumped off the step and ran down Higher Street, tittering to himself. Then he took a shot of the house, as though it was the Taj Mahal itself, and down the street he galloped. What report did he bring back home? Irish husbands never do a stroke of work, but sit in the sun drinking gin and tonic while indoors the wife swans about naked as God pleases. A curious race, no doubt about it. Next year I feared a hundred Japanese trespassers would infiltrate, cameras about their necks like hangmen's ropes.

Speer's Secret Garden

The retaken city of Berlin was the home of Albert Speer for twenty-seven years. He was confined in a place of imprisonment where the occupying powers had control turn and turn about. Albert Speer cultivated a garden only to see it destroyed when the Red Army contingent marched in. When they pillaged they did it thoroughly.

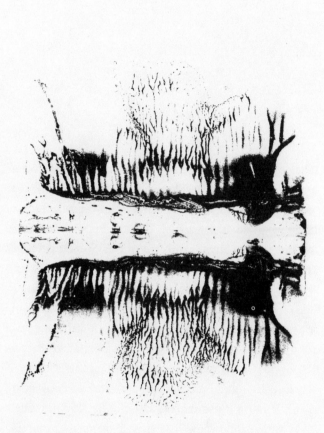

West View

We had passed it many times, the house hidden down a short twisty avenue. The address on the gate of the hidden house was West View. When it was being renovated some anagram genius had rearranged the temporary lettering, and had amused himself with Wet Wives. So we passed by.

Diagonally opposite, a new mansion had grown up behind an eight-foot estate wall with a spacious entrance defended by a large hardwood gate, also eight foot tall, to prevent dogs from befouling the yard. On a plaque was inscribed Beacon Hill, which looked to me like Bacon Hill, or maybe Rasher's Hall. It was a dog control.

Below the hill a bar restaurant had a half-door such as are found in horse stables, and a notice BAD FOOD. Or so my eyesight would have it, in a town famous for its cuisine. The sign read BAR FOOD.

I encountered John Heath-Stubbs with the photographer John Minihan at a function at Swansea and was emboldened to ask "What is it like, to be blind? Blind as a bat, in total darkness?"

"Well, not quite," he answered. "You live in a yellowish mist all the time."

"When you look at Minihan, what do you see?"

"A yellowish blur."

"Not a bad description of him," I said.

But Heath-Stubbs was helpless as a baby, led into the jakes by his protector.

Blindness is a state of helplessness, of being an infant again.

Incident on the Hill

One fine day, I detected a stout elderly woman leaning against a gatepost. On approaching her I saw it was a wheelie-bin waiting to be collected. All was blurred for the same problem. Men become women, they become garbage collections.

Days and hours vanish from sight. Six-day weeks become common, the unknown becomes familiar. Nearness and distance, night and day merge. So it goes for the semi-sighted. There is no continuity, here all is topsy-turvy.

On another occasion I was coming down the hill when I saw an old codger, quick-taken, who was relieving himself on the road verge. Hearing me approach he hastily adjusted his trousers and flopped onto the road and spreading his arms and rising up made off in the clumsy way that herons fly. He flew ahead until he reached a gatepost where he perched. Old codger become heron become gatepost.

So I may call this Blind Man's Bluff, so much of it is hallucination, a walking dream.

I believe that we are divided into two; the dreams and nightmares then become an unknown world, revealed to us. On awaking it disappears. We forget it except perhaps for the most scarifying nightmares that frighten the life out of us. This division of the self commences very early, in infancy when we can neither walk nor talk.

Saul Bellow refers to the hidden prompter, the unknown, unseen, and unheard-of prompter of writers. He was referring to the struggle for the right, the appropriate word, the only word that will do. The hidden prompter will apply to more than writing. The self divides against the self.

Or if you wish a return to infancy when the helpless one can neither walk nor talk, needs to be fed, put to bed, all part of helplessness. So where shall I begin?

Let me begin if you wish before the beginning, the children waiting to be born.

I was the third of four brothers, born in the county Kildare, taught to read by my mother who was a great reader herself, pushed around in a pram, a black hooded contraption shared by my brother who was two years my junior.

In this most funereal-looking thing we were pushed about no doubt marveling at the scenery, the cows, the walled estates, the marvels of an unknown world that was ours.

A Walk in the Dark

Blind men are hard to find, rare as hares, seldom-seen loners. In the twenty years spent in Kinsale I have encountered only two of this species. A hare on a by-road where cars and pedestrians are seldom seen. The hare had his back to me but escaped into a field when he heard my approach. When I came to the gate he had vanished, as they are prone to do.

One blue day out walking, when my sight improved, I came upon an elderly couple conversing at the end of their curving driveway. I offered some pleasantry about the blue of the sky overhead, the estuary below. The wife responded but the husband did not. I spoke to him but he remained silent. His wife had to say, "My husband is blind." He saw nothing of the estuary. He didn't see me, just a voice in the void that is blindness.

I rarely venture out of doors these days, spring and four degrees below freezing. I have become an indoor person, lie most of the day on the bed on a serape bought in 1961 in Mexico City by my wife's deceased father. It's like traveling through space and time, a magic carpet. I ruminate as Joyce did before me. The shattering daylight of no thought vanishes.

If I stand at the morning door a mist obscures both ends of Higher Street. Some days it intensifies, becomes murk, out of which a figure may emerge. I can't tell male from female, the unknown one from the known. The past comes closer and the present disappears. Time itself goes awry. Some days go missing. The hours are no longer consecutive, evening or morning . . . morning and evening merge.

1906 — 1989

Robinson Crusoe

When Robinson Crusoe, marooned for twenty-eight years on his island, dressed in the skins and fur of animals he had shot for the pot, sat on a bluff looking out to sea for the sail that never appeared, what thoughts passed through his mind?

Did his mind become empty as the years went by and he had nothing to think of but the daily grind of keeping himself alive, the daily chores, umbrella furled, fowling piece by his side, dog asleep, parrot on his shoulder, his mind troubled by the constant fear of the cannibals returning from another island with their trussed victims, the start of a horrible feast on the shore?

Little by little he began to forget his language. It slipped out of his mind, with nothing to read, none to talk to but parrot and dog, his memory grew feeble except for practical matters.

A Footprint in the Sand

SOMEWHERE JUST OUT OF SIGHT THE SAVAGES WERE HOWLING.

I wrote that before my eyesight began to go and it is in the nature of a prophetic preliminary for what follows. The lone man on the deserted remote island, his domestic arrangements, his fears. Was it Daniel Defoe who wrote the first book in English, a journal of rejection, a lone character who must invent a fortress out of the side of a hill? He had to pretend to be many men defending his fortress house.

He had no one to speak to. Communication with his fellow men and women cut off. Women absent. His condition is child-like, the prevalent chaos that precedes speech. It is an extraordinary book of several. In modern times few but forgotten criminals serving life sentences experience such solitude. Albert Speer in Spandau Prison serving twenty years feared to embrace his wife lest he compromise one of the friendly guards.

Modern writing, let us say, began with the *Anatomy of Melancholy*. Proust, you might say, is cut off from most readers in his class rigor. Joyce, *The Brothers Karamazov*, are excessively garrulous works, and can only be understood if you follow the argot, which tends to be outdated. Faulkner, whose original surname omitted the "u," ignored chronology. Eula Varner (Mrs. Snopes) and retired lawyer Gavin Stevens spoke in one voice, Faulkner in a fury of composition. Speech is reduced to only what his memory dredges up, anecdotal past and present merge. Blind Man's Bluff in repetition attempts to wed the blind man and the innocent that is the child.

AIDAN HIGGINS is the author of short stories, novels, travel pieces, radio plays, and a large body of criticism. His books include *Scenes from a Receding Past*, *Bornholm Night-Ferry*, *Balcony of Europe*, and *Langrishe, Go Down*, which was adapted for television by Harold Pinter.

SELECTED DALKEY ARCHIVE TITLES

FOR A FULL LIST OF PUBLICATIONS, VISIT:
www.dalkeyarchive.com

SELECTED DALKEY ARCHIVE TITLES